A New IMPROVED Santa

by Patricia Rae Wolff ✳ illustrated by Lynne Cravath

SCHOLASTIC INC.

New York Toronto London Auckland Sydney
Mexico City New Delhi Hong Kong Buenos Aires

For my mother, with love and hugs.
–P.R.W.

For Jesse and Emily, with love!
–L.C.

ISBN 0-439-57449-8

Text copyright © 2002 by Patricia Rae Wolff. Illustrations copyright © 2002 by Lynne Cravath. All rights reserved. Published by Scholastic Inc. SCHOLASTIC and associated logos are trademarks and/or registered trademarks of Scholastic Inc.

12 11 10 9 8 7 6 5 4 3 2 1   3 4 5 6 7 8/0

Printed in the U.S.A.   40

First Scholastic paperback printing, November 2003

Book design by David Caplan.

The text of this book is set in
Esprit Book.

One Christmas morning at the North Pole, Santa Claus looked
in the mirror and said, "The chimneys seemed smaller this year. I must be
getting fatter. My clothes are old-fashioned, and my 'Ho-ho-ho' is so-so-so
boring. My New Year's resolution is to become a new, improved Santa."

Mrs. Claus shook her head and settled into her rocker to read. "Yes,
dear," she murmured.

In **JANUARY** Santa Claus went on a diet. He ate salads. He ate bran. He snacked on carrot sticks and rice cakes and tofu.

"Look at me now — a new, improved, *slimmer* Santa," he said.

"Almost skinny," Mrs. Claus said with a twinkle in her eye. She edged toward the kitchen to throw away her stash of leftover Christmas cookies.

In **February**
Santa Claus exercised.
He jumping-jacked.

He jogged.

He did sit-ups
and stretches
and toe touches
(well, knee touches).

"Look at me, look at me now — a new, improved, *stronger* Santa," he said.

"Most impressive," Mrs. Claus said. She tossed his weights on top of the basket of blocks she was carrying. "I'll put these away for you in the workshop."

In **MARCH** Santa Claus changed his hair. He first dyed it red.

He then dyed it black.

He cut it and spiked it and sprayed it.

"Look at me, look at me, look at me now — a new, improved, *younger-looking* Santa," he said.

"Trendsetting," Mrs. Claus said, trying not to giggle as she brushed wisps of multicolored hair from his shoulder.

In **APRIL** Santa Claus changed his suit.

He tried bell-bottoms.
He tried leather.

He tried western

and retro and grunge.

"Behold a new, improved, *stylish* Santa," he said.

"Definitely dapper," Mrs. Claus said, squinting her eyes as she straightened his fish-shaped fuchsia tie.

In **May**, **June**, and **July**,
Santa Claus changed his glasses, hat, and boots.

In **AUGUST** Santa's "Ho-ho-ho" turned into booming shouts of "Yo, man" and "Cool" and "Rad."

"Maybe these will help," Mrs. Claus said, chuckling as she passed out earmuffs to all the elves.

In **SEPTEMBER** the children's letters started pouring in. "A new, improved Santa uses technology," Santa Claus said as he set up a computer. He copied letters. He logged lists. He typed and sorted and saved.

"Please notice I'm a new, improved, *cyber* Santa," he said . . . just before his computer crashed!

"Oh, dear," said Santa Claus.

"Don't worry," said Mrs. Claus. She went to the closet and opened the door. "I saved all the letters the old-fashioned way — in boxes."

In **OCTOBER** Santa Claus put the sleigh into storage.

He tested a helicopter.

He tested a truck.

He tried a motorcycle

and snowmobile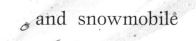

and plane.

He pulled up in front of the house and called
Mrs. Claus to come look. "See my new wheels."

"Truly innovative," Mrs. Claus said. She went to the barn to reassure the reindeer by shining up the old sleigh.

The day of the first **NOVEMBER** holiday parade, Santa Claus spiked his black hair. He waxed his red mustache and braided his beard.

He put on his psychedelic shirt, his skinny plaid suit, and his high-heeled cowboy boots.

Then he climbed into his roaring red rocket-copter and . . .

. . . with a wave of his cowboy hat, he was off.

"Introducing the new *me!*" Santa Claus called as he flew away
to show off a new, improved Santa to the children.

But the children didn't smile or cheer. Some frowned, some pouted.

And one little girl burst into tears and cried out, "Where's the real Santa?"
Most just stared — disappointed, dismayed, and downright unhappy.

A rejected, dejected Santa returned to the North Pole.
"The children don't like the new, improved me," he said.

Mrs. Claus closed her book. "Then we'd better get to work," she said, handing Santa Claus an Eggnog Power Smoothie.

They rewhitened his hair,
beard, and mustache.

They unpacked his old clothes and boots.

They hustled and bustled and
scrambled and scurried to change
new Santa back to old Santa
by Christmas.

On **CHRISTMAS EVE** Santa Claus climbed into his old-fashioned sleigh, dressed his old-fashioned way.

"Look at you now," Mrs. Claus said as she kissed him good-bye. "A new, improved Santa."

"But I'm not new and improved," Santa said. "I'm the same old Santa."
"Oh, no you're not," Mrs. Claus said with a smile. "You're *smarter*."